# Gloria Rand

# Fighting for the Forest

### Illustrated by

## Ted Rand

Henry Holt and Company · New York

Dad and I used to hike in a huge ancient forest. Dad said it had been growing forever, even before George Washington was born. My grandfather brought Dad to this forest when Dad was my age. Then Dad and I came to the forest together. Hiking there was a family tradition.

It was dark in the forest and quiet. There was a musty, woodsy smell I liked.

Fairy Slipper

Great Grey Owl

The paths and game trails were soft with layers of rotting needles, cones, and moss. We found animal tracks made by deer, elk, cougar, and even bear.

"Shhh. Don't move," Dad would whisper whenever elk or deer appeared. We'd watch them and they'd watch us. We shared the woods.

Elk

Cougar

Dad and I often stopped to rest on a gentle slope above a stream. We could tell by the matted-down grasses covering our resting place that deer sometimes rested there too. It was nice to sit where the deer had been. We felt right at home.

Porcupine

Raccoon

Clark's Crow

Nuttall's Woodpecker

The forest was full of tiny creatures. Chipmunks and mice scampered across our path and we saw beetles and sow bugs crawling in and out of the dirt. There were bats and all kinds of birds, such as owls, woodpeckers, blue jays, and Clark's crows, also called camp robbers. The camp robbers often swooped down from high up in a tree to take pieces of bread from me.

Chipmunk

Ground Beetle

Steller's Jay

I thought the forest would always be there. But one day, Dad and I discovered something strange. Blue marks had been sprayed on the trunks of all the bigger trees.

"What are these marks for?" I asked Dad. "What do they mean?"

"They tell loggers which trees to cut down," Dad said with a sigh. "What a shame, what a terrible shame. It looks like someone is getting ready to clear-cut this whole ancient forest, cut down every tree. Lumber could just as easily be harvested from younger trees that were planted to replace ancient ones that have been logged off in the past."

Great Horned Owl

Bat

"Are all the trees going to be cut down, even the little ones?" I asked.

"No, not the little ones. No one is going to bother cutting them down. They'll be smashed flat when the bigger trees fall," Dad said, frowning. "Our resting place, the one where the deer rested too, will be ruined. Most of the wildlife is going to be left homeless. And lots of fish will die when rain and melting snows fill the streams with mud from the exposed ground."

Opossum

Indian Paintbrush

Dad sat down on an old stump.

"Maybe we could stop the logging." I tried to cheer Dad up a little.

"Maybe," Dad agreed. "If we could get a conservation or environmental group to help us, it's possible."

"Why don't we do this, Dad?" I asked. "Why don't we tie ribbons around the big trees near the road to get everyone's attention? Then we could hold up signs that say SAVE THIS FOREST. We could get lots of people to help."

Dad thought my idea was pretty good.

Tiger Lily and Lupin

*Skunk Cabbage*

Starting the next day, Dad went to local environmental and conservation meetings. He wrote letters and called friends, asking for their support in an effort to stop the logging. Mom and I made stacks of signs and bought rolls and rolls of red ribbon.

After we finished making the signs, a whole bunch of volunteers met us at the forest. All day long we tied ribbons around the trunks of the big trees that grew next to the highway. There were so many trees that needed ribbons, we had to come back the next day to finish.

I tied the last piece of ribbon around the trunk of a tiny tree, one that seemed to be asking, "Hey, what about me?"

Then we held up the signs. People driving by honked their horns, waved, and yelled "Good luck!" It was exciting, and it got even more exciting when a TV van pulled off the road and a reporter came over to interview Dad.

That night we watched ourselves on the news. It was the first time I'd ever seen me on TV.

The next morning Dad got a call from the head of an environmental group, the people who had been helping us in our efforts to keep the forest from being cut down.

"I just learned," the woman told Dad, "that contracts, signed more than a year ago, give the timber company the right to cut down the trees. There is nothing anyone can do to stop them now. It looks like we've lost our fight to save this forest."

Leopard Frog

Two days later, Dad and I watched from a nearby ridge as old giants, still wearing their red ribbons, shook the earth as they hit the ground. The mountain air filled with the smell of pitch and crushed evergreen boughs. Diesel and gasoline fumes belched from trucks, bulldozers, and power saws.

As soon as the workers quit for the day, Dad and I climbed down to the logged-off area. There were only bulldozer tracks where the trees used to be. The forest darkness was gone. The animals and birds were gone. Only beetles and bugs were there, scurrying around trying to find a place to hide.

Dad and I stood still for a long time. We didn't talk, we just looked around.

"Where's the forest?" I finally asked. "Where has it gone?"

Bunchberry

After a while, we found another forest to hike in. This forest is farther away, but it too has huge trees, a woodsy smell, the dark quiet, and lots of wildlife.

"It's hard to believe that a place we cared about so much is no longer here," Dad said one day as we lay under a tree. "But thanks to efforts like yours, everyone is getting wiser about saving the environment. Let's hope this forest will be allowed to live forever."

"I hope it will, Dad," I said.

One thing I'm sure of, a forest is worth fighting for.

Black Bear Cub

# Trail Guide

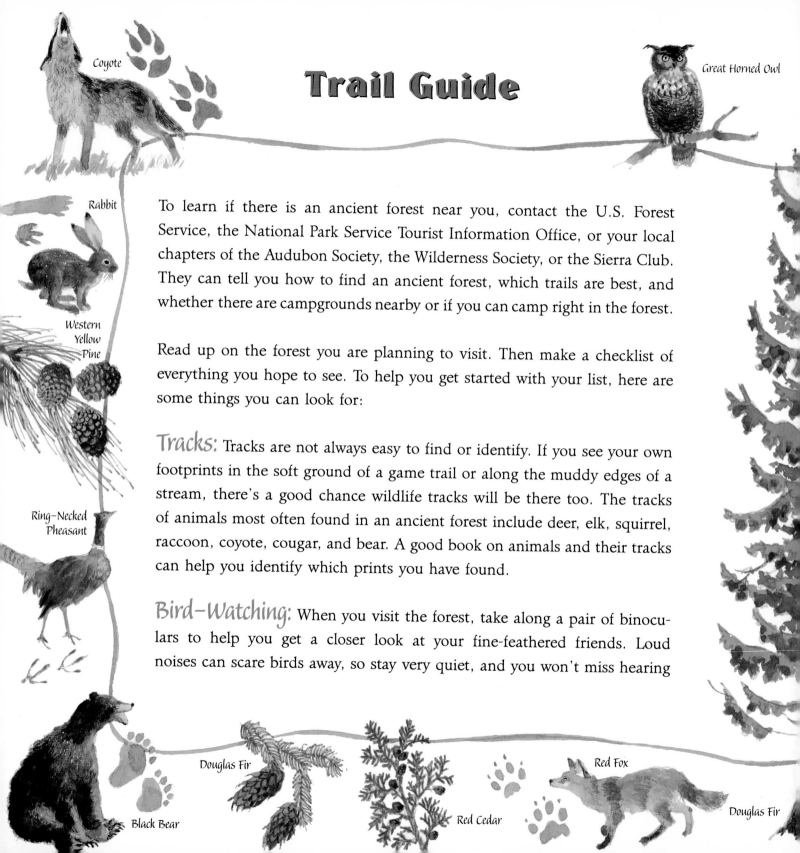

Coyote

Great Horned Owl

Rabbit

Western Yellow Pine

Ring-Necked Pheasant

To learn if there is an ancient forest near you, contact the U.S. Forest Service, the National Park Service Tourist Information Office, or your local chapters of the Audubon Society, the Wilderness Society, or the Sierra Club. They can tell you how to find an ancient forest, which trails are best, and whether there are campgrounds nearby or if you can camp right in the forest.

Read up on the forest you are planning to visit. Then make a checklist of everything you hope to see. To help you get started with your list, here are some things you can look for:

## Tracks:
Tracks are not always easy to find or identify. If you see your own footprints in the soft ground of a game trail or along the muddy edges of a stream, there's a good chance wildlife tracks will be there too. The tracks of animals most often found in an ancient forest include deer, elk, squirrel, raccoon, coyote, cougar, and bear. A good book on animals and their tracks can help you identify which prints you have found.

## Bird-Watching:
When you visit the forest, take along a pair of binoculars to help you get a closer look at your fine-feathered friends. Loud noises can scare birds away, so stay very quiet, and you won't miss hearing

Black Bear

Douglas Fir

Red Cedar

Red Fox

Douglas Fir

their different calls. If you listen carefully, you might even learn a few calls yourself.

Trees: The best way to identify a tree is by its leaves or needles and bark. Do you know the difference between a pine and a fir, or a cedar and a hemlock? A field guide will help you identify what you see. Taking pictures or making sketches of different trees is a good way to remember them.

Flowers and Bushes: In springtime, wild flowers of all kinds bloom in the forest. In the fall, bushes are loaded with berries. Some berries are good to eat, some are poisonous. Don't eat any berries unless you and an adult are absolutely sure what they are. The more common berries to look for are red or blue huckleberries, blackberries, salmon berries, and thimble berries.

The most important tools you can take into an ancient forest are your eyes and ears. Enjoy hiking, but also be sure to take time out to find a quiet spot where you can sit down to rest a while and watch and listen. Was that a deer you just heard?

Dedicated with great pride to our son, Martin Rand, who, along with other caring volunteers, tied ribbons around the trunks of trees in an ancient forest. This fight was lost, but the next fight was won, and an ancient forest stands in victory.

—————————————————

"There is a delight in the hardy life of the open. There are no words that can tell the hidden spirit of the wilderness that can reveal its mystery and melancholy of its charm. The nation behaves well if it treats the natural resources as assets which it must turn over to the next generation increased and not impaired in value. Conservation means development as much as it does protection."
—Theodore Roosevelt

Henry Holt and Company, Inc., *Publishers since 1866*
115 West 18th Street, New York, New York 10011
Henry Holt is a registered trademark of Henry Holt and Company, Inc.

Text copyright © 1999 by Gloria Rand. Illustrations copyright © 1999 by Ted Rand. All rights reserved.
Published in Canada by Fitzhenry & Whiteside Ltd., 195 Allstate Parkway, Markham, Ontario L3R 4T8.

Library of Congress Cataloging-in-Publication Data
Rand, Gloria.   Fighting for the forest / Gloria Rand; illustrated by Ted Rand.
Summary: When they find blue logging markings in the ancient forest where they like to hike, a boy and his father try to save the trees from being cut down. Includes information about how to find and enjoy ancient forests.
[1. Forests and forestry—Fiction.   2. Logging—Fiction.   3. Conservation of natural resources—Fiction.]
I. Rand, Ted, ill.   II. Title   PZ7.R1553Fi   1999   [E]—dc21   98-6610

ISBN 0-8050-5466-9 / First Edition—1999
The artist used transparent watercolor and grease pencil to create the illustrations for this book.
Printed in the United States of America on partially recycled acid-free paper. ∞
1  3  5  7  9  10  8  6  4  2